SCRUFF

STRIPES PUBLISHING LIMITED
An imprint of the Little Tiger Group
1 Coda Studios
189 Munster Road,
London SW6 6AW

A paperback original
First published in Great Britain in 2019

Text and illustrations copyright © Nicola Colton, 2019

ISBN: 978-1-78895-069-5

The right of Nicola Colton to be identified as the
author and illustrator of this work has been asserted
by her in accordance with the Copyright, Designs
and Patents Act, 1988.

A CIP catalogue record for this book
is available from the British Library.

Printed and bound in China.

STP/1800/0269/0419

2 4 6 8 10 9 7 5 3

Nicola Colton

JASPER
& SCRUFF

Stripes

Jasper was the type of cat
who knew what he liked.

He liked living on the top floor of a grand apartment building, which was so fancy it even had a doorman.

He liked having a large bookcase
full of impressive books, which
he had arranged by colour.

He liked his wardrobe, which contained bow ties in every pattern imaginable.

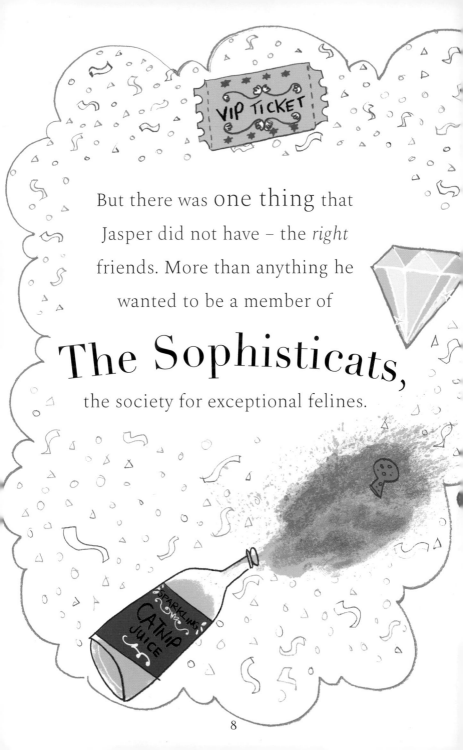

But there was **one thing** that Jasper did not have – the *right* friends. More than anything he wanted to be a member of

The Sophisticats,

the society for exceptional felines.

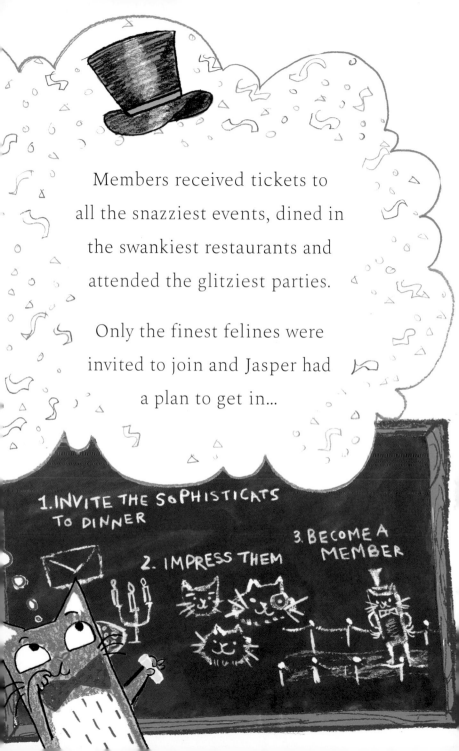

Members received tickets to
all the snazziest events, dined in
the swankiest restaurants and
attended the glitziest parties.

Only the finest felines were
invited to join and Jasper had
a plan to get in...

1. INVITE THE SoPHISTICATS
TO DINNER

2. IMPRESS THEM

3. BECOME A
MEMBER

Jasper waited ... and waited
for The Sophisticats to reply
to his invitation.

He was ironing his bow tie one
morning when something sharp
hit him on the back of the head.

Floating to the ground was a
handsome envelope with his name
printed on it in brilliant gold.

He picked it up and carefully opened it.

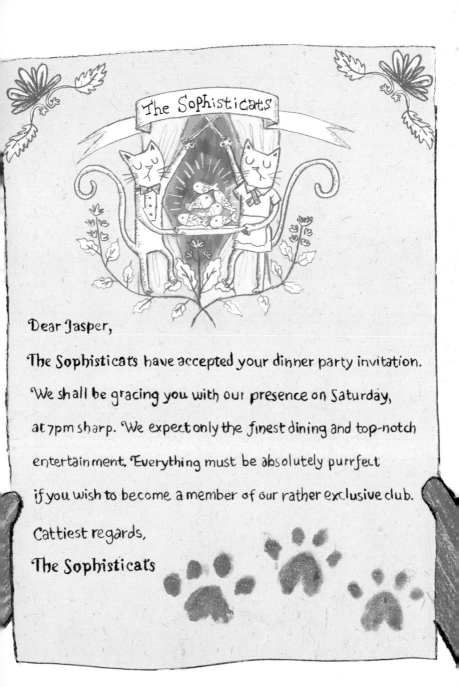

Dear Jasper,

The Sophisticats have accepted your dinner party invitation.

We shall be gracing you with our presence on Saturday,

at 7pm sharp. We expect only the finest dining and top-notch

entertainment. Everything must be absolutely purrfect

if you wish to become a member of our rather exclusive club.

Cattiest regards,

The Sophisticats

Jasper checked his diary. "But that's only two days away!" he panicked. With no time to waste, Jasper set to work...

He polished the silverware until it gleamed. He dusted his art collection. He fetched all the recipe books from his bookcase. He wrote a shopping list. He *even* had a bath.

The morning of the dinner party arrived.
Picking up his shopping basket, Jasper
headed off to Snootington High Street.

At the deli, Jasper counted
the holes in the cheese.

"No, this will not do at all.
Poke more holes in this Gouda,"
he told the shopkeeper.
"And I'll also have a wedge of your
stinkiest, bluest, tangiest Stilton."

In the fishmongers he measured the fish.

He listened to the bread rise at the bakery.

He walked around sniffing, poking and
squeezing things in the Food Emporium
before putting them in his basket.
Only the best would do.

On his way home, he took a shortcut through the park. Suddenly, he heard a peculiar noise behind him. A sort of panting sound...

He turned round.

There on the path, staring up at him, was something he did not like one bit.

It was a puppy.

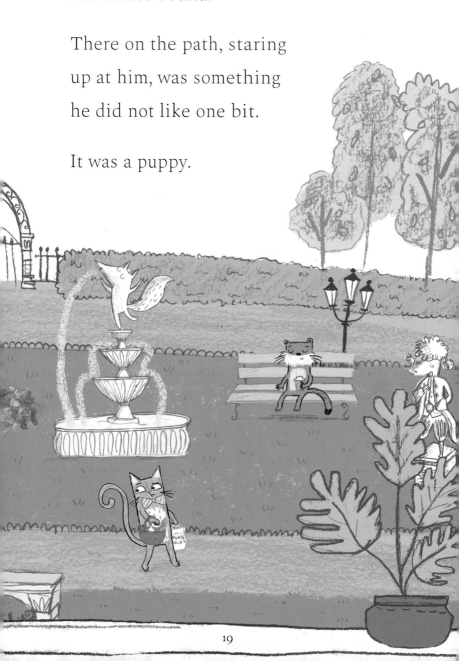

Jasper shuddered. Dogs were bad enough, but puppies... They were the opposite of everything he liked – noisy, unruly and worst of all, messy. He could not stand them!

The puppy tilted his head and gave Jasper a hopeful look. Then he leaped into Jasper's arms and gave him a BIG, SLOPPY LICK.

"Get off me!" Jasper cried,
putting down his bags and
wiping the drool from his
face with a silk hanky.

"Hello! I'm Scruff,"
the puppy yapped,
wagging his tail excitedly.
"What's your name?"

"Not interested," said Jasper.
He picked up his bags
and started to walk away.

Scruff followed.

"Not interested?

That's a funny name!

Do you like the park?

It's my favourite place!

It's great for games.

Do you want to play fetch?"

Before Jasper had the chance to reply,
the puppy leaped into a nearby flower bed.

He returned with a drool-soaked ball,
which he dropped at Jasper's feet.

"Great idea," said Jasper. He picked
up the slobbery ball with his hanky
and threw it as far as he could.

"*Fetch!*"

The puppy bounded off to get the ball...

...and Jasper quickly made his
way back to his apartment.
He closed the door with a click.

"Good grief, that little scamp
got mud everywhere," he tutted.
"Still at least I got rid of—"

Jasper looked down. The bags
of groceries slid from his paws
and thudded on the floor.

To Jasper's astonishment, Scruff had managed to follow him all the way home.

"You again? How did you get past the doorman *and* into my apartment?" he asked weakly.

"Hello! That was fun!" said Scruff, wagging his tail. He dropped the ball at Jasper's feet. "Do you want to play again?"

Jasper thought for a moment.
He picked up the slobbery ball
with his hanky.

Then he stepped out into the hallway
and hurled it down the stairs.

Scruff scampered after the ball and
Jasper followed quickly behind.

"Let's play another game," Jasper said, as the ball bounced down the front steps and rolled off down the street. "How about hide-and-seek? You go back to the park and count to a thousand."

"Aren't you coming too?" asked Scruff.

"Er, yes," said Jasper.
"I just need to grab my coat."

"OK, but you'll have to think of a good hiding place," said Scruff. "I'm brilliant at hide-and-seek."

Jasper rolled his eyes as he watched Scruff bound off towards the park.

Then he headed back upstairs.

Jasper placed the shopping bags on the
kitchen table, put on his chef's hat and
opened up a recipe book.

But as he reached for the eggs
he realized they were *broken*.

"How am I going to make my Salmon Soufleé now?" Jasper wondered aloud, as he wiped the goo from his paw.

Sighing, Jasper rubbed out Salmon Soufleé on the menu and wrote Salmon Surprise. He would just have to make something up.

He whizzed around the kitchen, chopping, stirring and sniffing. Finally, with the soup bubbling in the pan, the fish in the oven and the cake iced, he laid the table and lit the candles. He had just started to fold a napkin into a swan when—

Ding Dong!

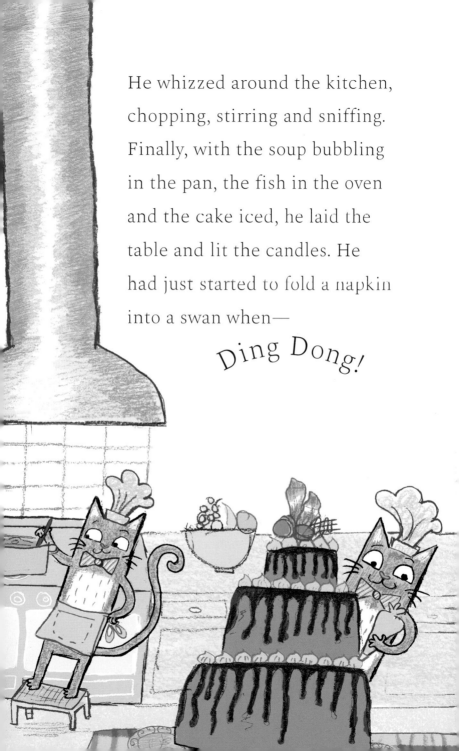

"They're here!" Jasper jumped.

There was no time for swans.
He straightened his bow tie
and opened the door.

"Lady Catterly, how wonderful to see y—"

"Yes, yes," she said. "Now, where's the dining room? I'm *positively* famished." She slung her fur coat at Jasper.

"Er, straight through here.
Please, do make yourself at home."

"I'm parched," Lady Catterly said,
seating herself at the head of the
table. "Run along now and fetch me
your best Sparkling Catnip Juice.
There's a good chap."

She gave her crumpled
napkin a catty glance
and scribbled something
in her notebook.

LICK
LICK

But before Jasper could reach the
kitchen, the doorbell rang again.

Ding Dong!

"Reginald! Oswald! How splendid
to see you b—"

"Jasper, my good man," Reginald said, rubbing his paws together as he strode into the hallway. "There's a chill in the air. Get me a hot chocolate, quick as you can!"

"Make mine a vanilla milkshake with a cherry on top," said Oswald, following behind.

"Chop, chop!" Oswald threw his cane
at Jasper, hitting him on the nose.

"Ouch!" Jasper yelped. "I mean, come
on through to the dining room..."

"Darling, I am still waiting on my drink,"
Lady Catterly called, as they entered.

"Be with you in just a moment,"
said Jasper, bowing low.

Jasper hurried into the kitchen to prepare the drinks. He poured some Sparkling Catnip Juice into his finest crystal glass.

He heated up a pan of milk and stirred
in some melted chocolate, before
tipping the mixture into a fancy mug.

Then he whipped
some cream until
his arm ached
and spooned
it on top,
followed by
marshmallows
and chocolate
shavings.

He scooped ice cream into a drinks
shaker, added a dash of milk and
shook it until it became a thick, frothy
milkshake. He poured it into a tall
glass and topped it with a cherry.

He placed all three drinks very, very
carefully on a silver tray.

He'd just stepped out into the
hallway when he stumbled over
something soft and *scruffy*.
The tray flew up into the air...

...and landed on the floor
with a tremendous *crash*.

Jasper stared down at the mess in
disbelief. A slobbery ball rolled across
the floor and stopped by his feet.

"Found you!" panted Scruff.
"Good hiding place! I searched all
over the park but you weren't there."

Jasper let out a long sigh. *How did that puppy get in again?* But there was no time for questions.

"Shh!" said Jasper, picking up Scruff and placing him in the bathroom. "Let's play the silent game. You stay in here and be quiet for the rest of the evening."

"Oooh, a new game!" said Scruff.
"I love games! Is there a prize?"

"Er, yes, something nice to eat,"
whispered Jasper.

He closed the bathroom door firmly
behind him and reached for his hanky.

"What was that
awful noise?"
cried Lady Catterly.
"And where is my
glass of fizz?"

"Where's my hot
chocolate?"
whined Reginald.

"Hurry up, old chap, I need my milkshake," moaned Oswald.

"Be with you in just a moment!" called Jasper. "I just had a slight mishap."

"Well, really," said Lady Catterly.

"Mishaps are not something

The Sophisticats approve of."

Jasper quickly remade his guests' drinks
and carried them into the dining room.

"Finally," said Lady Catterly.

"About time," said Reginald.

Buuuurrrp! went Oswald.

Jasper brought out
the first course.

"May I present, Creamy Chowder
with Catnip Croutons," he said,
puffing out his chest.

Lady Catterly took a sip and handed
the bowl back to Jasper. "Ugh, this is
very bland. It needs more seasoning."

"Far too watery," said Reginald.
"Blend it with some cream."

"That was barely a mouthful," said
Oswald, after guzzling it down in
one go. "Fetch me some more!"

Jasper collected their bowls
and hurried back into the kitchen
to pep up the soup.

His guests tasted their soup for the
second time. "Passable," they said.

Jasper brought out the next course.
*How can they possibly find fault with my
Salmon Surprise?* he thought.

"Too many bones," said Lady Catterly.

"Too chewy," said Reginald.

"Noh 'nuff saush," said Oswald,
his cheeks bulging with food.

Jasper was beginning to wonder if joining The Sophisticats was worth all this trouble. "Of course. I will fix your dishes right away," he muttered.

As the cats tucked into their second helping, Jasper crossed his fingers. He was so jittery he had barely touched his own food.

"Just about edible," said Lady Catterly, as the others licked their plates clean.

Jasper hoped he could turn things around with his famous Salted Caramel Cake. *Everyone loves that!* he told himself as he took the empty plates through to the kitchen.

But as he stepped into the room, he let out a horrified gasp. The caramel buttercream had disappeared, and the sponge was now covered in a fine coating of hair and drool.

Beside the cake stood Scruff,
panting happily.

"Hello! I was silent for ages so
I thought the game must be over,"
said Scruff. "I found the prize!
It's yummy!"

"What have you done? My beautif—"
Jasper began. Then a smile spread
across his face as he thought about
his guests' behaviour so far.

"Let's see what they have to say
about dessert," he said.

He took a length of rope from a drawer and looped it round Scruff's leg. "Sorry, Scruff, but I need you to stay put until my guests are gone," Jasper told the puppy, as he tied the other end of the rope to the table.

"Oh, OK," said Scruff. "Is this a new game?"

"Er, yes," said Jasper, as he closed the door.

Jasper brought the hairy disaster of a cake to the table and set it down with a flourish.

"Dessert is served!"

"What *exactly* is this?" said Lady Catterly. "It looks a frightful mess!"

"It's Gateau à la *Scruff*," said Jasper. "Haven't you heard of it? It's the Queen of Belgium's favourite, you know."

"Of course I've heard of it! Gateau à la ... er Scruff, yes," she replied, taking a big bite.

"Mmm... A fond favourite of mine too," said Reginald. "It's served at *all* the fashionable parties."

"Why, I had it just the other day," said Oswald.

"Of course you did," said Jasper.

"And, remind me again, what are these stringy bits?" asked Lady Catterly, holding up one of Scruff's hairs.

"Oh, that's finely spun sugar," said Jasper. "It's made by the best confectioners in Belgium. Very exclusive *and* expensive."

"*Delicious*," said Lady Catterly.

"Very moreish and wonderfully,
er, moist," agreed Reginald.

"Just as good as the last time I had it,"
said Oswald.

"I'm so pleased you like it," said Jasper.
"Now, it's time for the entertainment."

He seated himself at the piano and
began to play his favourite tune.

"Too slow," said Lady Catterly, drumming her claws on the table.

"Borrrinnnng," said Reginald, with a yawn.

"Play us something more jazzy.
Chop chop!" said Oswald,
throwing his fork at Jasper's head.

As Jasper's eyes began to focus again he noticed that Scruff was now under the dining table, chasing his ball in circles. The rope Jasper had tied him up with was trailing behind him, wrapping round and round the guests' feet.

Jasper finished his tune and gave a bow.

"Well, I think we have seen and heard quite enough, Jasper," said Lady Catterly. "And I am not at all convinced that you are Sophisticats material."

"I agree." Reginald nodded. "Jasper is not up to snuff."

"Indeed," said Oswald. "And if we leave now we can make the show at the Velvet Theatre."

They stood up to go...

Splat!

Lady Catterly landed face
first in the remaining cake.

Crash!

Reginald stumbled into
the table and knocked
over one of the candles,
setting his hat on fire.

Boing!

Oswald bounced off the sofa and
found himself swinging from the
chandelier by the seat of his trousers.

"My fur is all matted with cake!"
wailed Lady Catterly.

"My hat has melted!" gasped Reginald.

"I'm going to fall!" cried Oswald.

There was a loud ripping sound
and he landed bottom first in
a bowl of cream.

Scruff appeared from under
the table, wagging his tail.

"A puppy!" they yowled together.

"I can't believe you've let one of those disgusting beasts in the house!" said Lady Catterly. "Mark my words, you will NEVER, *EVER* be a member of The Sophisticats."

"I second that," said Reginald.

"Yes, I ... eh, quite agree," said Oswald, blushing as he tried to hide the hole in the back of his trousers.

"Well, I can't think of anything worse than being a member of The Sophisticats," said Jasper. "And he's not a beast, his name is Scruff."

"Scruff?" said Lady Catterly in a faint voice. "Like the cake?"

"Oh yes!" Jasper grinned. "Scruff was a great help with the cake."

"Scruff ... helped?" she said, clutching her throat.

Reginald and Oswald stood mouths agape, turning a sickly green.

Jasper nodded. "He did a great job of licking off all the buttercream."

The three cats stumbled over each other as they hurried out of the door.

Jasper could still hear their screeches echoing down the street as he untangled Scruff.

"Well, it was, erm, interesting meeting you, Scruff," said Jasper, showing him out. "Now I must go and clean up. Time for you to head home."

"OK," said the puppy, his eyes large and watery. "Right, then... Bye."

Jasper sat down at the piano and
breathed a sigh of relief. He'd had
a lucky escape, thanks to Scruff.
Those cats were horrid! So why did he
have a funny feeling in his tummy?

PLONG!

Jasper hit several keys at once.
Had he been just as horrible to Scruff?
He ran to the door and flung it open.

"*Scruff!*" he called.

"Hello," said Scruff, in a small voice.

"Oh," said Jasper. He looked down at the doormat to see the puppy sitting there. "You're still here."

"I don't have anywhere to go,"
said Scruff.

"You don't have a home?"

"No ... not really," said Scruff.
"I've been sleeping in the park."

"Well, there's still lots of food left," said
Jasper. "Perhaps you could do me a *big*
favour and help me finish it?"
He flicked his tail encouragingly
towards the door.

"*Yummy!*" said Scruff,
and he bounded inside.

As Jasper prepared the food, he could
hear Scruff moving things around in the
dining room. Swish! Thud!

Puzzled, he poked his head
round the kitchen door.

"Er, Scruff?" said Jasper, as he watched
the puppy drag a large cushion off the
sofa. "Feel free to make yourself at home.
But can I ask what you're doing?"

"It's a surprise," panted Scruff.
"Come back in ten minutes."
He dragged another cushion
off the sofa. Swish! Thud!

Jasper folded his arms to
stop himself from putting the
cushions back in place. "Er, OK..."

When Jasper returned with a tray piled high with Salmon Surprise and a freshly baked cake, he was met with a surprising sight.

"Oh, Scruff!" he gasped. "It's lovely!"

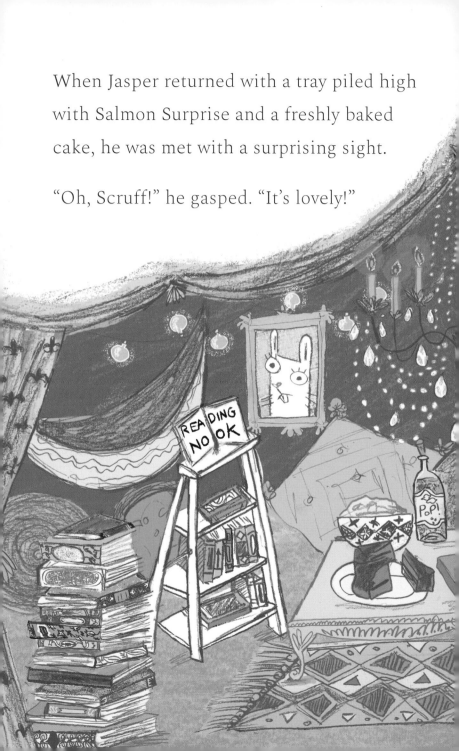

Scruff had turned the cushions
and blankets into a cosy fort.

"Why don't you come inside?"
said Scruff.

Somehow, Jasper reflected as they talked and ate, *my cooking tastes better than ever before. And I can't remember the last time I had so much fun...*

With their tummies full of food, Jasper and Scruff were both soon rubbing their eyes and yawning.

"Why don't you stay with me, Scruff?
I've got plenty of room," said Jasper.
"You can sleep in here for now until
we find you a proper bed."

"Thank you!" Scruff leaped into
Jasper's arms and gave him a
BIG, SLOPPY LICK!

Scruff curled up on some cushions and
Jasper pulled a blanket over him.

"Goodnight, Scruff," he whispered.

Smiling, Jasper tiptoed across the
room and clicked off the light.

It seemed he had found the
right type of friend after all.